BATMAN
THE BRAVE AND THE BOLD ™

TERROR ON DINOSAUR ISLAND!

Adapted by Jake Black
Based on the teleplay by Steven Melching
Batman created by Bob Kane

Grosset & Dunlap
An Imprint of Penguin Group (USA) Inc.

GROSSET & DUNLAP
Published by the Penguin Group
Penguin Group (USA) Inc., 375 Hudson Street, New York, New York 10014, USA
Penguin Group (Canada), 90 Eglinton Avenue East, Suite 700,
Toronto, Ontario M4P 2Y3, Canada
(a division of Pearson Penguin Canada Inc.)
Penguin Books Ltd., 80 Strand, London WC2R ORL, England
Penguin Group Ireland, 25 St. Stephen's Green, Dublin 2, Ireland
(a division of Penguin Books Ltd.)
Penguin Group (Australia), 250 Camberwell Road, Camberwell, Victoria 3124, Australia
(a division of Pearson Australia Group Pty. Ltd.)
Penguin Books India Pvt. Ltd., 11 Community Centre, Panchsheel Park,
New Delhi—110 017, India
Penguin Group (NZ), 67 Apollo Drive, Rosedale, North Shore 0632, New Zealand
(a division of Pearson New Zealand Ltd.)
Penguin Books (South Africa) (Pty.) Ltd., 24 Sturdee Avenue,
Rosebank, Johannesburg 2196, South Africa

Penguin Books Ltd., Registered Offices:
80 Strand, London WC2R ORL, England

The publisher does not have any control over and does not assume any responsibility for author or third-party websites or their content.

Library of Congress Cataloging-in-Publication Data

Black, Jake.
Terror on Dinosaur Island! / adapted by Jake Black.
p. cm.
"Batman: The Brave and the Bold."
ISBN 978-0-448-45340-8 (pbk.)
I. Batman, the brave and the bold (Television program) II. Title.
PZ7.B52893Te 2010
[E]--dc22
2009017637

ISBN 978-0-448-45340-8   10 9 8 7 6 5 4 3 2 1

CHAPTER 1

Few villains were as frightening as Gentleman Ghost. He was a ghost, after all. As such, it made perfect sense that he would plan a big robbery during the Day of the Dead parade. A night when everyone was dressed in spooky costumes. Riding his ghostly white stallion, Gentleman Ghost intended to escape with two large sacks filled with money.

Batman and Plastic Man ran across the rooftops, following Gentleman Ghost's trail. As Gentleman Ghost turned down an alley, the two heroes jumped down in front of him. Batman threw a small explosive pellet at the horse's feet, scaring it. The horse reared backward, causing Gentleman Ghost to drop the bags of money. When Plastic Man saw how much money was in the bags, he became very excited.

Batman was on Gentleman Ghost's trail while Plastic Man went after the money. Although now a super hero, Plastic Man was once a thief himself. He stared longingly at the bounty Gentleman Ghost left behind, and stretched his arms out to catch as much cash as he could.

"Oh, you beautiful dinero. Moolah! Cabbage! Spondoolicks!" Plastic Man shouted to the coins and bills that now surrounded him.

Batman caught up to Gentleman Ghost in a graveyard. The Caped Crusader was surprised to see an open grave with a tombstone reading *HERE LIES BATMAN*. From behind, Gentleman Ghost blasted Batman with a bolt of energy, sending him into the open plot. Gentleman Ghost stood above Batman and laughed.

Batman leaped from the grave and landed a punch square to Gentleman Ghost's jaw. The evil spirit revealed his true form.

"Nth metal knuckles," Batman explained. Nth metal was the only substance that could have an effect on the supernatural.

Batman put Gentleman Ghost in Nth metal handcuffs. Plastic Man arrived and his body was full of the stolen cash. Batman told his friend he had to return the money to the bank. Disappointed, Plastic Man knew it was the right thing to do.

CHAPTER 2

Deep in the heart of the Atlantic Ocean, a large yacht carrying a party of wealthy people sailed on the peaceful water. A few minutes later, the celebration came to an end. In the distance, several large pterodactyls flew toward the yacht. They were carrying a group of gorillas led by the villain Gorilla Grodd! A brilliant ape, Gorilla Grodd planned to take over humanity

and rule the world. Gorilla Grodd landed and boarded the yacht.

"Your day is done, humans! The age of the ape is at hand!" Grodd declared, wearing his powerful mind-control helmet. He then revealed a strange ray gun and blasted a wave of energy at one of the passengers. The ray gun transformed the man into a caveman!

In the sky high above the troubled yacht, Batman and Plastic Man flew in the Bat-Jet. Plastic Man was apologizing for trying to keep the money that Gentleman Ghost had stolen. He was interrupted by the alarm of a distress call. Batman determined the call was coming from the yacht on the ocean below.

"Hang on," Batman said as the Bat-Jet flew toward the yacht.

"Are you seeing what I'm seeing?" Plastic Man asked Batman. "Because I'm seeing gorillas . . . riding pterodactyls . . . with harpoon guns . . . stealing a boat."

Batman realized what was happening. "It's Gorilla Grodd," he said.

"It's messed up is what it is," Plastic Man said.

Batman tried to steer the Bat-Jet closer to the boat. But Gorilla Grodd and several of his soldiers jumped on their pterodactyls and flew toward the Bat-Jet.

Gorilla Grodd and his troops fired energy beams at the Bat-Jet. Grodd knew that Batman was the only human who could defeat him. Batman had to be stopped. Grodd activated his mind-control helmet and focused his thoughts on Batman.

"You are under my control. You cannot resist.
Succumb to Grodd," Gorilla Grodd said quietly.
Inside the Bat-Jet, Batman's eyes grew wide.
His mind was under Gorilla Grodd's control!

CHAPTER 3

Batman was in a trance. His mind was now controlled by Gorilla Grodd. Panicked, Plastic Man tried to get Batman to snap out of it.

"Bats? Not a good time for a nap!" Plastic Man shouted as he shook Batman.

The Bat-Jet veered out of control. Plastic Man had no idea how to fly the plane, and Batman was out of commission. Plastic Man shook Batman one more time, desperate to free him from Grodd's control.

Finally, Plastic Man's efforts paid off. Batman regained consciousness and took control of the Bat-Jet. But it was too late. Grodd fired a missile at the plane and destroyed it! Batman and Plastic Man escaped as the Bat-Jet burned up. Batman reached out to Plastic Man as they fell and grabbed his friend's wrists and ankles. Plastic Man stretched his body into a glider, and the two heroes landed safely on a nearby island.

The island was a beautiful paradise, full of lush jungle life. Batman scanned the area, trying to determine where he and Plastic Man had landed.

"Dinosaur Island," Batman said. "A mysterious land where the normal laws of nature don't apply."

Confused, Plastic Man asked, "What makes you say that?"

"That dinosaur," Batman responded. He pointed at a massive Tyrannosaurus rex roaring ferociously nearby.

The dinosaur spotted them and began to chase Plastic Man and Batman in the hopes of having a hero sandwich for lunch!

Plastic Man ran ahead of Batman and attempted to escape by weaving his stretchy body through the jungle. However, his foot got caught under a branch on the ground and stretched his leg like a rubber band.

Plastic Man snapped backward, right into the dinosaur's waiting jaws!

"Ew, gross! Dinosaur germs!" he shouted.

The Tyrannosaurus rex spit him onto the ground and Plastic Man leaped to his feet.

"Grab on," Plastic Man said.

Batman clung to Plastic Man as he stretched his arms and swung from branch to branch. He swung over a ravine, leaving the dinosaur in the distance behind them. The dinosaur roared in defeat across the ravine. Batman and Plastic Man were safe.

CHAPTER 4

The heroes peered over the cliff's edge into the valley below. There they saw a large compound filled with gorillas, cavemen, and stolen yachts. It was Grodd's hideout. Plastic Man stared at the stolen luxury boats in awe.

"We're taking Grodd down," Plastic Man said.

"Don't get any ideas about the money on

those yachts," Batman warned him.

Gorilla Grodd's compound was a maze of security cameras and laser trip wires. Plastic Man stretched his body and weaved his way through the defenses.

"They didn't call me the 'Eel' for nothing," he whispered.

Batman quietly followed after his friend, avoiding the traps set by Gorilla Grodd. He swung on a Batrope, sailing safely over the trip

wires. He landed next to Plastic Man, who stood smiling next to a large tree.

"See, Bats, no problem," Plastic Man said. He leaned back onto the tree. Suddenly, alarms rang loudly throughout the compound. Plastic Man had accidentally pushed a hidden button inside the tree. Batman shook his head. Grodd's forces would be there momentarily. It was time to fight.

Gorillas riding atop pterodactyls swarmed

overhead. Angry apes riding on the backs of dinosaurs charged them from within Grodd's fortress. Batman and Plastic Man took their positions, ready to battle whichever enemy arrived first. To their surprise, it was Gorilla Grodd himself. He was riding a dinosaur and carrying his caveman-creating blaster, the E-Ray. Batman and Plastic Man glared at the villain.

"You're a long way from Gorilla City, Grodd," Batman said.

Gorilla Grodd patted his weapon.

"My E-Ray evolves humans into intelligent apes. It only needs one more test, and I see

two new volunteers," Gorilla Grodd said.

"Not interested," Batman said, throwing several smoke pellets at the ground.

The explosive pellets startled some of the dinosaurs. The gorillas moved in on Batman and Plastic Man. Surrounded, Plastic Man twisted his rubbery body around two trees. A gorilla slammed into his stretched-out torso and bounced backward as if fired from a slingshot.

Meanwhile, Batman and Gorilla Grodd fought. Grodd tried to take control of Batman's mind. But Batman blocked it by focusing on his enemy. Batman used his speed as an advantage against the lumbering gorilla. Grodd appeared to be no match for the Caped Crusader.

A pair of gorillas grabbed Plastic Man's

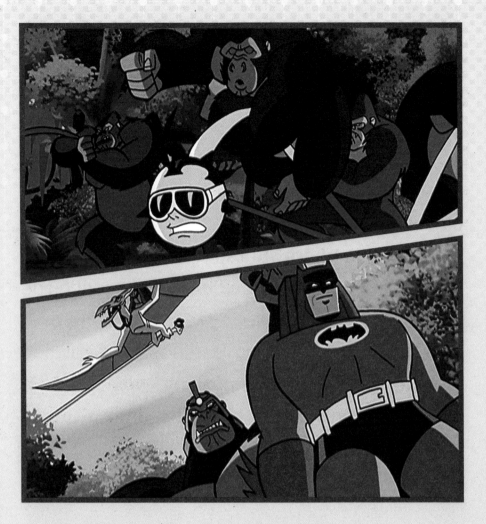

wrists and ankles and stretched him tight. He called out to Batman and the distraction gave Gorilla Grodd the advantage he needed. With incredible strength, Grodd grabbed Batman's leg and slammed him into a tree. Grodd lifted Batman's unconscious body and carried him inside the compound. The two gorillas released their grip on Plastic Man, sending him flying through the air like a rubber band.

Plastic Man landed hard on the other side of the jungle. He quickly pulled himself up from the ground.

"Nice going, Plas," he said to himself. "Way to get one of your only friends in this lousy world captured."

"Hang in there, Bats!" Plastic Man called out. He stretched his flexible legs through the jungle, stepping between trees, crossing over rivers, and moving around dinosaurs. Batman needed his help, and nothing would get in his way. Soon he was outside Gorilla Grodd's compound, ready for action.

CHAPTER 5

Batman awoke to discover his arms and legs bound in cuffs. Fortunately, he had several lock picks hidden inside his gloves. Sneaking out a pick, Batman unlocked his shackles and was free from the restraints. Gazing around, he saw that he was in a high-tech laboratory. Gorilla Grodd entered the laboratory and saw that Batman was free.

"You amuse me, Batman," Grodd said.

Batman smiled. "My only goal is to send you back to the zoo!"

Gorilla Grodd laughed and turned his back to the Caped Crusader, focusing his attention on his computers. Grodd explained that he and his fellow gorillas had fixed the problems with the E-Ray. It was now ready to turn all of humanity into gorillas. Several gorillas swarmed around Batman, holding him still. Gorilla Grodd laughed as he activated his E-Ray, and pointed it directly at Batman!

Outside Gorilla Grodd's compound, Plastic Man stretched his body into a giant spring. He bounced over the security wall, landing inside Grodd's fortress. When a pair of gorilla guards moved in close, the stretchy hero changed his appearance to look like a shovel. Hiding next to a real shovel, Plastic Man hoped the apes wouldn't notice him. Not realizing one of the shovels was actually Plastic Man, the gorillas began using the tools to clean the grounds.

A short time later, Plastic Man resumed his quest to save Batman. He spit out some of the

dirt and grime he'd tasted while pretending to be a shovel. He stretched his legs, wrapping them around the corner of a massive building. In the distance, Plastic Man could see Gorilla Grodd's laboratory. He knew that Batman was being held captive inside. It was time to prove he was a hero by saving his friend.

Plastic Man used his legs to launch his body toward the laboratory. His aim was a little off, however, and he slammed into the building's outside wall. He slithered through a nearby window that led into a room inside Gorilla Grodd's laboratory.

Plastic Man was shocked to see the room was full of gold, money, and precious jewels. He

had never seen so much money in one place. His jaw dropped all the way to the floor. He wanted the money—badly.

"No! Stay strong. I'm not going to let Batman down. Not going to . . ." Plastic Man said to himself, not very convincingly.

His mind raced back to the night when he robbed the chemical plant. Before he was

Plastic Man, he was Patrick "Eel" O'Brian, a common thief who worked for a villain named Kite Man. One night years ago, Kite Man and his thugs used large kites to fly inside a massive chemical plant. The crew of thugs broke into the plant's safe. Kite Man, O'Brian, and the other thieves filled several bags with money from the safe. But they were interrupted when Batman came crashing through the roof into the plant.

O'Brian grabbed bags of money and ran. He grabbed a kite and started flying toward the window. Batman couldn't let O'Brian escape with the money. He threw a Batarang at the

thief's kite, damaging it. O'Brian plunged from the air into a vat of chemicals that transformed him into Plastic Man.

He remembered that, while Batman had caused him to fall into the chemicals, the Caped Crusader had also pulled him out. There was no denying that Batman had always been a friend to Plastic Man. He remembered that Batman

stayed with him while he was in the hospital, recovering from the chemical bath. Batman even helped him get out of prison.

Now, gazing at the money, he completely forgot about Batman. The stretchy hero dived into a large pile of cash, rolling around in it like a pig in the mud.

He grabbed handfuls of the treasure and started swallowing it! As it had before, Plastic Man's body expanded as he ate the fortune.

Having eaten all of the money in the vault, Plastic Man burst through the door and ran down the hall. His body was a lumpy, awkward blob. Plastic Man had overstuffed himself. Still,

he was determined to save Batman! Plastic Man finally arrived outside Grodd's laboratory. He broke through the lab door and saw Batman. He called out to his friend.

"I got your back, Bats! Told you I wouldn't let you down," Plastic Man said.

Batman turned to face him. Plastic Man spit out a stolen diamond in shock as Batman grunted. He had been transformed into a gorilla!

CHAPTER 6

Gorilla Grodd was celebrating his victory. Batman had become an ape, Plastic Man was not a threat, and he was about to turn every person within five hundred miles into a gorilla. Grodd activated a massive version of the E-Ray.

"Tell me you have a plan," Plastic Man whispered to Batman.

"I always have a plan," responded the costumed primate.

Batman ran toward Gorilla Grodd and slammed into the larger ape.

Several gorilla soldiers attacked Plastic Man. A gorilla hit Plastic Man hard in the stomach, causing a couple of diamonds to shoot from his mouth. The precious jewels hit one of the gorillas, knocking him to the ground. Plastic Man realized he had a new weapon to use against Gorilla Grodd's army: the gold and jewels in his belly!

The lab computer announced that Grodd's gigantic E-Ray would fire in less than two minutes. Batman battled Gorilla Grodd, trying desperately to shut down the E-Ray. Several gorillas entered the room, surrounding Batman and Plastic Man.

"I can't believe I'm doing this," Plastic Man said disappointedly.

He punched himself in the stomach, blasting a gold bar from his mouth. The gold smashed into a gorilla's face, and Plastic Man raced toward Batman.

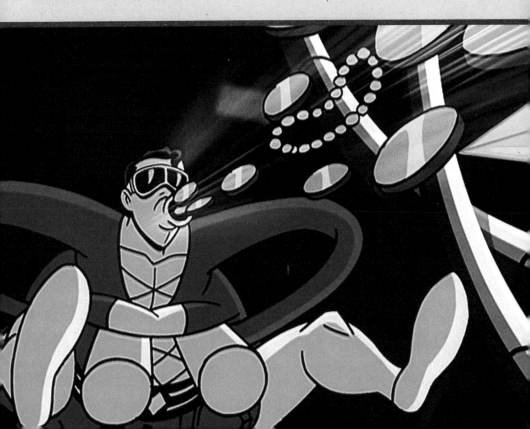

Batman and Gorilla Grodd wrestled each other near the E-Ray controls.

"Bad monkey. No banana," Batman grunted.

Gorilla Grodd grabbed Batman around the waist and shouted, "Monkeys are not apes!"

Batman twisted free from Grodd's grasp and flipped the evil gorilla to the ground. Carefully, Batman climbed up a web of cables connected to the computer. Batman was almost to the E-Ray control button, but Grodd was close behind.

High atop the laboratory, Batman reached for the E-Ray switch.

"I think not," Gorilla Grodd said, grabbing Batman by the ankle.

Grodd pulled Batman back, preventing him from shutting down the E-Ray. The two apes pulled each other from the E-Ray's main controls, swinging between the massive power cables.

"10 ... 9 ... 8 ..." the computer voice counted down.

"Too late, Batman," Grodd said.

"7 ... 6 ... 5 ..." the computer continued.

Firing gold, money, and jewels from his mouth, Plastic Man fought his way through Grodd's forces. High above him, he saw Gorilla Grodd and Batman falling. Plastic Man stretched his body to reach the E-Ray switch, but it was no use. The computer counted down the final seconds: "4 . . . 3 . . . 2 . . . 1 . . ."

The E-Ray burst to life, blasting out an incredible stream of energy.

The E-Ray energy surged out of Grodd's laboratory and spread across Dinosaur Island. Inside the laboratory, the energy faded. Plastic Man was shocked to see that Batman was no longer an ape. Next to Batman stood a large man. Gorilla Grodd had been turned into a human being! His plan had backfired.

"Human? No!" Grodd yelled.

Batman smiled and said, "Looks like human ingenuity beats ape intellect once again."

Confused, Plastic Man asked Batman what had happened. "Why weren't we turned into apes?"

Batman revealed that he had reversed the

E-Ray's emitter matrix when Grodd wasn't looking. Instead of changing humans into gorillas, the E-Ray transformed every ape within five hundred miles into a human. It also saved the people Grodd had transformed on the yacht. Plastic Man was impressed with his friend's brilliant work. He watched happily as

the police arrived and took the human Grodd away to jail.

Inside his jail cell, the former Gorilla Grodd hung from a metal bar. Although human in appearance, Grodd was still a gorilla at heart. Peeling a banana, Grodd promised that he would one day get his revenge on Batman. Someday soon, Grodd would escape from prison and do what was necessary to return to his natural gorilla form.

Batman and Plastic Man were ready to leave Dinosaur Island.

"I rounded up all the money," Plastic Man said. "You want to count it?"

The Caped Crusader smiled at his friend. "No, I trust you."

Batman turned and walked away. Plastic

Man pulled out one last diamond he'd hidden in his ear. He tossed the jewel away and followed Batman. He realized that earning Batman's trust was more valuable to him than money, and he didn't want to disappoint his friend.